CORNELL DYER AND THE CALCIUM DEFICIENT BONES

An *Adventures of Cornell Dyer*
supernatural mystery

Denise M. Baran-Unland

In collaboration with
Timothy Baran

Illustrated by Sue Midlock

ISBN: 978-1-949777-47-5

This book is lovingly dedicated to the reader, whoever you might be.

If you cannot get rid of the family skeleton, you may as well make it dance. — George **Bernard Shaw, "Immaturity"**

CONTENTS

PROLOGUE

She glanced up from her stack of papers and looked at the wall clock. Fifteen more minutes.

Then she could collect her third grade students' unit tests on the human body.

She stretched her thin, crooked fingers – achy and stiff from holding a pen so long – and brushed back a lock of wispy white hair.

A few noises broke the room's silence – like the tick tick tick tick tick of the timer as it wound down.

Like the tapping of Davy's left foot, a sign he was thinking deeply.

Like the scritch of Janey's teeth against the metal of her pink pencil eraser, a sign she was thinking deeply.

Like Timmy clearing his throat over and over and over again, a sign he was thinking deeply.

Like the scrape of the legs of the old maple wood chair across the old mastic tile, for Carl never could sit still.

Only Susie made no noise. She just twirled a pigtail and bit her lip, signs she was thinking deeply.

BING!

All seventeen students set down their pencils.

The end-of-the-day bell rang through the intercom.

"Class," she said. "Please set your tests on my desk as you leave."

The students rose. They shuffled to the front of the room. They placed their tests on her desk and then dashed out the door.

She picked up the papers, straightened them, and then slid the stack into her duffle bag. Then she roamed the room,

She lined up every desk and chair with the seams of the tile.

She clicked off the overhead projector.

She tugged the pull ring dangling from the world map and gently retracted it into place.

She picked up the chalkboard eraser and erased her stick figure drawings. She set the eraser in the chalkboard tray and placed the pieces of chalk next to it.

Then she snapped off the lights and hung up her work.

The next day, the first period students waited and waited and waited for their teacher. Finally, Craig and Jenny went to the principal's office.

"Why are you here?" Mr. Principal demanded. "Why aren't you in class?"

"Our teacher is gone," Craig said.

"She never showed up," Jenny added.

Mr. Principal leaned over his desk and called into the next room. "Miss School Secretary, please print dittos for the fifth grade science students. And please sit with them in class.

"Yes, Mr. Principal," Miss School Secretary said.

Soon, Miss School Secretary was leaving the school office with Craig, Jenny, and a handful of dittos. That's when Mr. Principal reached for the phone.

"Is this the world famous supernatural super sleuth Cornell Dyer? Do you specialize in Amulets, Fortune-Telling (with and without cards), Ghost-Hunting, Horoscopes, Numerology, Palm-Reading, Potions, Séances, Spells, Vampire-Slaying, controlling zambie populations, and deactivating Moravian pink goblins and cold whispers? Great! I need a substitute teacher. Please come right away!"

.

CHAPTER ONE: INSIDE THOSE BATTERED, TATTERED WALLS

It was late afternoon when Cornell Dyer drove his motor home past the "Welcome to Sunnystorm, Pennsylvania" sign.

What a long, long drive!

Traffic jams!

Stops for breakfast, morning snack, lunch, first afternoon snack, and second afternoon snack.

Road constructions!

Plus, read up on Sunnystorm, just in case he stumbled upon a supernatural mystery.

He learned Sunnystorm wasn't a big town. In fact, the town only had one school for grade school and high school.

But Sunnystorm was a nice town with nice

people who earned plenty of money. But it wasn't always that way.

Sunnystorm used to be a poor town. Sunnystorm struggled to survive – until it's luck changed.

Today Sunnystorm was full of people with plenty of money. And these people wanted to pay Cornell lots of money. People with lots of money were Cornell's favorite kind of people.

That's why Cornell agreed to teach when his real job was solving supernatural mysteries.

Cornell turned on his wipers to swish away the pattering rain. He also lowered the visor to keep the sun out of his eyes.

Sunnystorm, Cornell snorted. They sure got the name right.

He read each street sign as he passed it. Where was Hitchcrook Lane? Ah, there it was, just past the traffic light.

Soon Cornell was turning into the school parking lot right behind the garbage truck, which drove to the rear of the building. Cornell, on the other hand, stopped his very large motor home right in front of the school. The building had three stories and was made of old yellow bricks. It had tall vertical windows with old, stained window shades, the kind of shades that teachers pulled down by white plastic rings. Only a few cars remained in the parking lot. The rain had already stopped. The sun was still shining.

Cornell stepped out of his motor home. He walked to the front door and then walked inside. He didn't even wipe his wet sneakers on the mat.

To the right was the school office with a sign: "Please excuse our remodeling."

Wooden ladders leaned against the walls and stood in the middle of the hallway.

Old sheets covered things he couldn't see.

He saw stacks and stacks and stacks of fresh lumber, maple wood, he deduced from its color and grain.

He saw patches of fresh olive green paint covering the old dingy olive green paint.

Pieces of the floor were missing, where the old dull brown mastic tile was being replaced with new dull brown mastic tile.

The heavy air smelled of paint and tile glue.

Cornell turned to the office and knocked on the old maple door.

"Come in," a voice called out.

Cornell turned the creaky knob and stepped inside. The receptionist's office was empty of people. But it was full of cheerful, full pf green cacti, purple orchids, and delicate white ginseng. A door to his left was closed. The metal plate said, "School Secretary."

But the inner office door was open, and

the light was on.

The man at the desk looked up. He had a square face, smiling eyes, crooked teeth, and thinning hair. He also wore an expensive suit.

Now Cornell didn't wear suits. Cornell only knew the principal's suit was expensive because he paid attention to the clues: the cashmere cloth, the gold thread in the handmade buttonholes, the sparkling diamond buttons.

Cornell wore faded and patched blue jeans, a light blue T-shirt stretched over his barreled chest, and his colorful patchwork blazer over that. His T-shirt read, "Eat, drink, and be scary." His curly black hair looked as if he hadn't combed it in days – which he hadn't. Because Cornell was too busy solving supernatural mysteries.

"Are you the principal?" Cornell called.

"Yes," Mr. Principal stood. "Are you Cornell Dyer?"

"Professor Cornell Dyer," Cornell corrected.

"Ah, yes. Professor. Please come in."

Cornell noted dingy walls, faded green cushions, and faded paisley carpet.

He noted nicked arms and legs on the maple wood chair, the nicked maple wood of the principal's desk, and the nicked maple wood of the many picture frames.

"Forgive our mess," Mr. Principal smiled

and set a book over his papers. "We're remodeling our school."

Cornell sat on the chair and the springs squeaked. "Tell me about the job."

Mr. Principal sat and folded his hands. "We need you to teach science until the science teacher returns."

"What should I teach?" Cornell asked.

"Whatever you like," Mr. Principal said. "As long as it's science."

"For how long?"

Mr. Principal picked up a rubber band and rolled it between his fingers. "Until she returns."

"And you'll pay lots of money until she returns?"

"Of course, Professor. We pay all of our staff extremely well. We have an assistant principal, a receptionist, a secretary, a nurse, a cafeteria manager, three lunchroom workers, and homeroom teachers for all twelve grades, and teachers for all the subjects. We spare no expense when it comes to educating our two hundred and thirty-two students. In fact, every student gets twelve years of piano lessons and his or her own private piano."

"Can I see the classroom?"

"Of course, Professor." Mr. Principal stood and held out his hand. "The classroom is on the second floor, second door to the left."

Cornell shook Mr. Principal's hand.

Mr. Principal led Cornell to the hall. "Thank you again for helping us out."

"Sure," Cornell said.

Mr. Principal went back inside the office. Cornell heard the door lock.

Very strange, Cornell thought as he walked down the hall.

Old, dented metal lockers lined the halls. He saw an old-fashioned gymnasium to his left and a new-fashioned indoor swimming pool to his right. He heard the clang of old pipes and the hum of the central air conditioning.

He reached the stairs. He looked out the window. He saw a large running track, large basketball courts, large tennis courts, a large football field, a large baseball field, and an eighteen-hole golf course.

Cornell climbed the old wooden steps to the second floor. His footsteps echoed loudly in the nearly empty school. As he reached the second floor, a door flew open, and a man's head poked out.

The clean-shaven man wore thick glasses, a yellow cardigan, and a wide orange bowtie. His shiny black hair was slicked back with Billo-Cream.

"Oh, I'm sorry," the man said with a wide smile. "I didn't see you."

"Who are you?" Cornell asked.

"I am the history teacher," Mr. History

Teacher said. "And who are you?"

"I am Professor Cornell Dyer. I will be teaching science here for..."

"Well, I must get going." He switched off the light and shut the door. "Enjoy your tour."

Mr. History Teacher started for the stairs. Then he stopped. Then he turned around. He smiled again, waved, and said in a Peter Lorre voice, "Gooood niiight."

And then he was gone.

Cornell continued to the science classroom. But he felt as if someone were watching him.

Being a supernatural super sleuth, Cornell was right. He just didn't know it.

For Cornell did not see another classroom door silently opening. He did not see a teacher poke his head out. He did not see the eyes of this teacher meet the eyes of Mr. History Teacher, who peered around the corner. He did not see them nod to each other.

Finally, Cornell reached the science classroom. He jiggled the doorknob. The room was locked. So he peered through the glass window into the dark room.

Every desk and chair lined up with the seams of the tile.

The overhead projector stood on its stand, ready for the next day's classes.

A ring dangled from a short string of the

rolled up wall map.

The chalkboard was wiped clean. The eraser was in the chalkboard tray and the pieces of chalk rested next to it.

An old skeleton hung from a pole in the front corner of the room, next to the windows. As Cornell's gaze wandered to the window shades, he felt the skeleton's eyes look at him – so Cornell looked back.

Actually, the skeleton didn't have any eyes, just eye sockets. But they were watching Cornell.

Cornell rubbed his own eyes. He must be sleepy. Or hungry. That is why his eyes were playing tricks.

Except the skeleton didn't want him to go. Cornell could feel it in his own bones. He saw it in the commanding eye sockets and steady gaze.

So Cornell stared back. Maybe the skeleton wanted to tell him something.

As a supernatural super sleuth experienced in solving supernatural mysteries, skeletons often talked to Cornell. But if this skeleton had a message, Cornell wished it would hurry up and talk. It was past his dinnertime.

But the skeleton did not speak, at least not with words. Cornell felt as if the skeleton had grasped his mind with its bony clawed hands and was pressing the words into his brain.

Cornell rubbed his eyes again. The skeleton's hands hung by its side. So Cornell hurried down the hall, down the stairs, and out the door. He couldn't wait to heat up a big can of beef stew. He couldn't wait to listen to his favorite Wagnerian opera. He couldn't wait to get a good night's rest.

But Cornell found an envelope tucked underneath his windshield wiper.

Inside the envelope was a note and a key to the Milton Hotel.

The note said, "Your stay is on us. Thank you for helping us out." From the school board at Sunnystorm School.

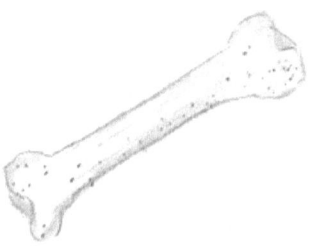

CHAPTER TWO: OLD AS BONE

Fifteen minutes.

That's how early Cornell Dyer arrived at the science classroom the next morning.

Because he needed to switch on the overhead projector, so it was ready to use.

Because he wanted to check the amount of chalk on the ledge.

Because he must lower the world map.

And because Cornell really wanted to examine the skeleton before his students arrived.

So he did – with his SkeleGlass 182, the best type of magnifying class for studying classroom skeletons.

Cornell walked all around the poor skeleton with that magnifying glass. But he didn't touch it, afraid he might break it.

The skeleton's bones were thin and pitted. One hand drooped by its side. The other was pinned up, as if it were waving.

And it was definitely watching Cornell.

As Cornell turned away, the sockets grabbed his eyes and...

Seventeen students filed into the room, and Cornell moved to the desk.

Every boy had neatly combed his hair to one side.

Each sleek ivory button on each boy's shirt was properly buttoned, and each shirt was tucked into the waistband.

Each pocket held a tortoise shell comb.

Each leather shoe was nicely polished.

Each girl's hair was neatly braided or pigtailed or ponytailed or tucked behind their ears with tortoise shell or ivory barrettes.

Cornell decided to teach the same subject – skin and bones – to all the grades so he wouldn't have to work too hard.

The students paid attention and answered all his questions. They squinted from the glaring sun glaring. They shouted over the teeming rain.

The loudspeakers crackled. Today was pizza pie day at Sunnystorm School, Miss School Secretary announced.

So at lunchtime, Cornell stacked half a dozen pizza pies on his plate. He also grabbed three chocolate cupcakes and a tall glass of milk.

Then Cornell sauntered to the teacher's lounge. He heard lots of laughing and talking. When he entered the room, all laughing and talking stopped.

Cornell caught three words: "old as bone."

The teachers smiled at him and introduced themselves. Cornell could not remember all their names. He didn't care.

When one is a great supernatural super sleuth, one doesn't bother with names. A brain will only hold so much information, Cornell's brain was full of supernatural clues and where to buy a giant hamburger with pickles.

The spacious lounge had plenty of maple wood tables and maple wood chairs. So Cornell easily found a place to sit. As he stuffed his mouth full of pizza, he studied the teachers.

They finished each other sentences and "talked" with finger points, head nods, and grunts.

Mr. Math Teacher spoke the most. He was tall with a long neck and a gravelly voice. He wore a diamond-studded watch and cufflinks.

Mrs. Librarian huddled in her chair with her cashmere sweater draped over her shoulders. Her eyes peered at her magazine through her tortoiseshell bifocals. She ate a tuna sandwich with one hand. She absently twirled her abalone necklace with the other hand.

Miss English Teacher graded homework with a tortoise shell red pen while she nibbled carrot sticks. She'd pinned her hair back with smooth ivory combs studded with glittering diamonds.

A maple wood bookshelf in the back held boxes and boxes and boxes of dominos.

Bored, Cornell stuffed the last of his pizza crust into his mouth. He left his tray on the table and wandered into the hall to search for clues. He stopped at the long maple wood trophy case. It was full of awards, plaques, and framed newspaper clippings.

One clipping announced the school's opening seventy years ago. The school had opened with two hundred and thirty-two students. He remembered Mr. Principal's words:

We spare no expense when it comes to educating our two hundred and thirty-two students.

Very strange, Cornell thought.

Cornell saw awards for the school's football team, the basketball team, the track team, the baseball team, the swim team, and the golf team.

He saw awards for best educator of the year, best principal of the year, best librarian of the year, best school nurse of the year, best school secretary of the year, best receptionist of the year, and best cafeteria manager of the year.

But most of the awards were science awards.

Just one teacher won the science awards: Miss Bethany Ann Calloswick.

She won seventy years of awards for teaching science. Framed newspaper clippings showed her holding awards.

In some photos, she had well-styled blonde hair and smooth skin.

And in others, she had wispy white hair and thin, wrinkled skin.

In fact, she looked...

"As old as bone," Cornell whispered.

Were those teachers talking about Miss Bethany Ann Calloswick?

And her eyes looked very familiar to Cornell.

But – how?

The bell rang. Cornell headed back to the classroom.

Cornell arrived just as his students walked through the door. He headed straight for the chalkboard and then stopped short, scratching his dirty curls.

The skeleton was gone.

The students were scraping the legs of

the old maple wood chairs against the tile.

Books thudded against the old maple wood desks as students dropped them.

The students freely laughed and chattered since Cornell had not started class.

Mr. Principal walked in the room.

"Professor, how is the teaching coming?"

"Fine," Cornell said.

"Good," Mr. Principal said. "We might need you to teach for a couple of weeks until we find the science teacher."

"You haven't found her?" Cornell asked.

"No," Mr. Principal said.

"Aren't you worried?" Cornell asked.

"Not at all," Mr. Principal said.

Mr. Principal left. Cornell turned to his class.

Now, Cornell hadn't prepared for any of his classes, so the students kept correcting his mistakes.

And he wound up drawing a skeleton on the chalkboard because the classroom one was gone.

"Tendons connect muscles to bones," Cornell said, touching his drawing with his pointer.

Emily raised her hand. "You mean ligaments, Professor."

"Your nerves," Cornell drew an imaginary line with his pointer, "respond without thinking to outside stimuli."

Jamie raised his hand. "You mean reflex, Professor."

Cornell whirled around. "Did I ask you?

No one answered.

"Now," he pointed again, "Your white blood cells help build new bone blood."

Cathy raised her hand. "You mean bone marrow, Professor."

Cornell slapped the pointer on the board. "And the digestive system moves through your entire body."

Alan raised his hand. "You mean the circulatory system, Professor.

Cornell whirled around again and whacked the pointer on the desk three times.

The students jumped.

"Young man," Cornell thundered. "When I'm hungry, I feel it from head to toe."

The students laughed.

"You're funny," Alice said with a giggle.

"Quiet!" Cornell ordered. "Use your lungs to keep your bones still, too."

Victor raised his hand. "Don't you mean muscles, Professor?"

"Detention!"

Cornell grabbed a note pad and a ball point pen and started scribbling.

At lunch, a very annoyed and thirsty Cornell stomped to the teacher's lounge to buy an orange drink from the pop machine.

He stopped short in the doorway. All the boxes of dominos were missing.

Very strange," Cornell thought as he pushed his nickel into the machine.

He slurped and thought all the way back to the science classroom.

After the final bell rang, Mr. Principal's voice crackled over the loudspeaker.

"Professor Dyer, please come to the office."

Cornell was hungry, thirsty, tired, and ready to for a big dinner at the Milton Hotel. But he plodded to Mr. Principal's office.

Mr. Principal shut and locked the door and then took his seat behind his desk.

"Professor, how is the teaching coming?"

"Fine," Cornell said.

"Are you sure? We're paying you a lot of money to teach."

That's when Cornell noticed the photos again. They were all of Mr. Principal and Miss Bethany Ann Calloswick.

Eight grade gradation. High school graduation.

Distributing science fair ribbons.

Dedicating the remodeled gyms, classrooms, and track field.

But in other photos, Miss Bethany Ann Calloswick was there but hidden.

Mr. Principal's wedding photo, where she sat at a table in the back, eating her dinner.

A concert in the park, where Mr. Principal sat with his friends, where she sat in the back, sipping a drink.

In some photos they looked young. And in some photos she looked old, and he looked like he did today.

Cornell heard a rumble. Beyond Mr. Principal's window, the garbage men were driving up to the dumpster.

Cornell had an idea.

"I will prepare harder for class," Cornell stood. "I'll head back to the classroom now."

"Good," Mr. Principal stood, too. "We believe in the best education for our students. A well-prepared teacher is an excellent teacher. I'll let you out."

Mr. Principal walked to the door, reached for the doorknob – and missed it.

Very strange, Cornell thought.

"The doorknob used to be in another place," Mr. Principal said with a little smile. "I was a little confused. As you know, we're remodeling."

"Of course," Cornell said.

Cornell hoped his classroom was still open. He'd left half a can of orange drink in there.

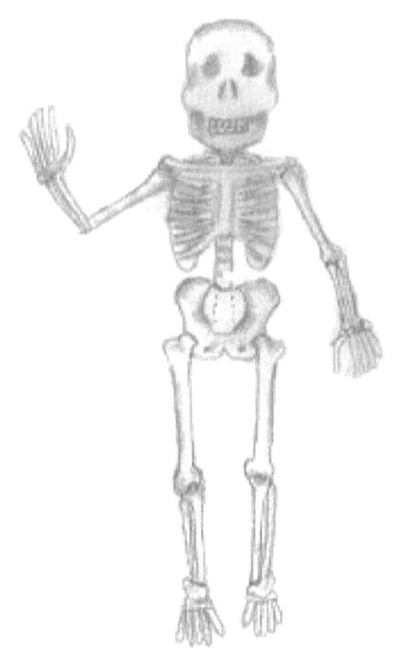

CHAPTER THREE: SKELETON IN THE ROOMS

But the science classroom was already locked for the night. Cornell scowled. Half a can or orange drink – wasted.

But maybe...

Cornell searched in all his pockets.

Past all the ketchup packets.

Past the mayonnaise packets.

Past his lucky goblin foot, his pet salamander, and his emergency ghost flashlight.

Finally, he found it – Skelly, his new skeleton lock picker.

Skelly looked like a white glow-in-the-dark toy found in cereal boxes.

"Hi, Professor," Skelly said. "Need to get into a room?"

"Shhh." Cornell pointed to the classroom.

Skelly glowed a happy green. He hopped onto Cornell's hand, He stretched his spindly fingers waaaaaay out and slid them inside the keyhole.

After a few clicks, Skelly gave Cornell the A-OK sign. Cornell turned the knob. The door swung open. Skelly jumped into Cornell's T-shirt pocket.

Sunset was a few hours away. So Cornell had plenty of light. Cornell sat on the edge of the maple wood desk and slurped the rest of his orange drink.

Then Cornell examined every corner, nook, and crack of the science classroom.

But he only found dust, crumbs, tiny particles of odd debris, and one dead fly.

He examined the world map and found a clue – faint marks on the continent of Africa.

Cornell grabbed his Map Magnifer 589T from a pocket inside his blazer. Cornell held the special glass over Africa. He saw little circles and scribbles.

The circles and scribbles were faded, as if someone had circled and scribbled a long, long, long time ago.

Cornell also saw marks on other places and continents, too. But most were on Africa.

Very strange, Cornell thought.

Cornell slipped the Map Magnifier 589T back into his pocket.

He turned his attention to Bethany's desk.

Nothing strange here. Just Cornell's empty orange drink cans scattered across the top.

Cornell opened the long drawer. Pencils with gold bands around the erasers. Red pens with abalone caps. Tortoise shell pencil sharpeners. A tortoise shell ruler.

No clues here. Cornell closed the drawer and then opened the top, right-hand drawer.

He found a stack of old, spiral-bound notebooks with faded, dusty covers. But the notebooks didn't lie flat. Now THAT was strange.

So he pulled them out. There lay a dusty stack of photographs in cheap metal frames.

Some photos were black and white. Others were hand-colored.

But they featured a young Bethany and a young man. They wore khaki knickers, flannel shirts, tall boots, and helmets. One photo had these words written across it: "Our safari."

Well, no clues here either.

Cornell replaced the photographs and shut the drawer. He opened the last two drawers. Empty.

It was getting dark. Cornell needed to explore the rest of the school. Skelly locked the door.

But Cornell didn't find any clues.

The history room was boring.

The math room was confusing. The art room was a dizzy blend of colors, shapes, and ivory sculptures.

The English room was divided into eight sections.

Each classroom had a skeleton. Only Cornell's classroom, the science classroom, didn't have a skeleton.

These skeletons weren't old and brittle. They looked new, sturdy, and as sleek as ivory.

Very strange, Cornell thought as he climbed to the third floor. Very strange, very strange.

The entire third floor was an auditorium. It had a large maple wood stage. It had two hundred and thirty-two pianos.

A skeleton stood in one corner of the auditorium.

Atchoo!

Cornell looked down. His shoes were covered in ivory chalk dust. Then he felt a drop on his forehead. He looked up. Was the ceiling was dripping?

Cornell pulled out his ghost flashlight. .

Ghost flashlights are the best flashlights for supernatural sleuthing. Only the sleuth can see the beam of light. Everyone else sees a dark room.

Cornell saw wet spots across the ceiling. He felt more drips.

Why was the roof leaking if the school were being remodeled? Why paint the walls and put in new floors without fixing the roof first?

Very strange, Cornell thought as he walked down the stairs. Very strange, very strange.

Next up – the school gym. The gym, too, was very strange.

The maple wood floors looked old and scuffed. The paint was dingy and stained. A few ceiling tiles were missing, too.

But the gym was filled with gleaming stationary bicycles and weight machines. The gym had speed bags, medicine balls, and exercise mats.

It didn't make sense.

He headed for the pool.

Even in the dark, Cornell saw the shimmery clearness of the water. He saw the newness of its blue and white tile. The pool was enormous.

Then Cornell saw it.

The defect was small. But supernatural super sleuths are trained to notice even the smallest details.

Way in the corner in the shallow end...

Right above the water was a little heart drawn in waterproof marker. In the center of the heart was J+A.

Cornell snorted.

Young love, he thought.

On his way out, Cornell stopped by the door to read the bronze plaque: "Donated by the Wonderbuilt Family. Keep your head above water and your dreams on the deep end."

Below the plaque was a sepia photo.

It had a man in a dark suit.

It had a woman in a flowered dress and flowered hat.

And it had twin girls, about seven, in long dresses with wide bows around their waists and in their hair.

The frame was maple wood, old and nicked.

No clues here, either.

He left.

The cafeteria had shabby walls and a shabby floor. It also gleaming new stoves, new refrigerators, new freezers, and new sinks.

The laminate on the maple wood tables didn't have a single fingerprint.

Not one metal leg had scratches or rust.

Not one maple wood chair had a scuff mark or worn spots.

Very strange, Cornell thought for the hundredth time that night.

He headed to Mr. Principal's office – and heard banging and clattering.

Cornell peered out a window. But it was just two garbage men in caps and uniforms. They were emptying the school's trash into their truck.

Mr. Principal's office was the same.

It still had dingy walls.

It still had faded green cushions on the chairs and nicked maple wood arms.

Mr. Principal's desk was still old and nicked – and so were the maple wood frames.

The paisley carpet was still faded.

Cornell inspected every corner, nook, and crack, but all he found was dust, crumbs, tiny particles of add debris, and two dead flies.

Now for the filing cabinet.

Cornell flipped through all manilla folders for the assistant principal, a receptionist, a secretary, a nurse, a cafeteria manager, three lunchroom workes, and homeroom teachers for all twelve grades, and teachers for all the subjects.

Finally Cornell came to the oldest and dustiest folder of them all. The folder belonged to Miss Bethany Ann Wonderbuilt.

He flipped through the paperwork.

Was "Wonderbuilt" her maiden name?

Was "Calloswick her married name? If so, then where was her husband?

Cornell heard the familiar rumble of garbage cans rolling down the hall. Time to go!

Quickly, Cornell pulled his ballpoint pen and little notebook from his T-shirt pocket and jotted down Bethany's address: 311 Reed Street.

As Cornell hurried out of the office, he noticed Miss Receptionist's plants were gone. Part of the remodeling?

Soon, Cornell was driving to the Milton Hotel. He couldn't wait to order a 56-ounce steak and a couple of double baked potatoes with extra butter and sour cream.

CHAPTER FOUR: THE CITY THAT WAS A LITTLE TOO PERFECT

The next day was Saturday, so Cornell didn't have to teach. So it was a good day to finally explore Sunnystorm.

Cornell spent a couple of happy hours driving around in his motor home while the sun shone brightly, and the rain pattered off and on.

Everything Cornell saw looked crisp, clean, and alive with activity,

Every road – whether it was on a wide street, large hill, or winding driveway, was freshly paved.

Cornell saw spacious golf courses and landscaped trails for walking.

A crystal clear river ran through the middle of the town. Majestic bridges gracefully went up and down to let the barges and the tugboats tooting in the distance to glide to the other side.

Train whistles tooted as gleaming trains clacked over the tracks.

Cornell drove through the neighborhoods.

He saw sprawling homes on expansive estates with lush green grass and colorful flower gardens.

He saw whistling mailmen delivering the mail and petting friendly, purebred dogs on their heads.

He saw hardworking garbagemen emptying trash and tipping their caps as people walked past.

Sunnystorm's downtown was filled with tall building of the grandest architecture: theaters, an art museum filled with ivory sculpture and a natural history museum with a wild animal exhibit, and stores that sold furs, diamond and abalone jewelry, music stores with piano sales, and game stores with sales on dominos.

Every store boasted exciting sales in their windows: tortoise shells combs for a quarter, diamond rings and abalone necklaces for ten dollars and mink coats for twenty dollars.

Very strange, Cornell thought.

He passed women walking briskly into stores, their heels clicking the sidewalks, or stopping at windows to gawk at the diamond rings, abalone necklaces, tortoise shell combs, and mink coats.

People wore expensive, tailored clothing; fur coats; and leather jackets. They drove expensive, flashy, freshly waxed sport cars.

Girls walked out of stores carrying their packages and giggling with each other.

Boys stood on street corners chatting about their favorite sports teams.

Businessmen held meetings at outdoor cafes.

One of those men was Mr. Principal.

So Cornell parked his motor home in a parking space that said, "reserved for motor homes" and headed to the café, whose name Cornell couldn't pronounce because he couldn't speak French.

"Professor!" Mr. Principal stood and waved. "Please join us."

Cornell ambled to Mr. Principal's table and took the empty chair. Mr. Principal handed Cornell a large menu.

"Professor, meet Mr. Superintendent, who sits in his office and does the nonimportant work," Mr. Principal said with a grin. "And meet Mr. School Board President, who's as useless as they come."

They chuckled at Mr. Principal's jokes.

"Please," Mr. Principal added. "Order as

much as you like. It's my treat." He turned to the other men. "This is Professor Cornell Dyer, world-renowned supernatural super sleuth. He's the one filling in for Bethany."

"Ah, yes," Mr. Superintendent said. "Will you stay in Sunnystorm until we find Bethany and continue teaching science to the younger grades?"

"Not sure," Cornell said.

The waitress set a large orange drink in front of Cornell. He reached for it and gulped half.

Wait a minute, Cornell thought in mud-gulp. I haven't ordered yet.

"Don't rush him," Mr. School Board President said. "He needs time to think it over."

"True," Mr. Superintendent said. "Important decisions take time. So, Professor, what do you think of our downtown? We're building a new school building right in the heart, next to all the museums."

Cornell took a long, thoughtful slurp of his nearly empty drink. "Why remodel the old school if you're building a new school?"

"Because it takes many years to build a new school," Mr. School Board President said. "The new school is for the future."

The waitress brought out Cornell's food: A tall stack of pancakes topped with whipped cream and strawberries, along with four large slices of bacon, four large sausage links, a carafe of maple syrup, and another tall orange drink.

"How about our neighborhoods – have you seen those?" Mr. Superintendent said.

"Yes," Cornell said, chewing with his mouth open. "They're very nice."

"You know, Professor, if you take the teaching job," Mr. School Board President said, "there's a great house for sale on Reed Street."

Mr. Superintendent nodded. "You'd probably get a good deal on it. It's been empty for a while."

Cornell quickly finished the breakfast he didn't order and a third large orange drink. But when he returned to his motor home, he did not drive directly to the Milton Hotel for an afternoon nap.

He drove back to the neighborhoods and looked for Reed Street. As Cornell steered his motor home up and down the hills, he did not see any homes for sale.

But he did find 311 Reed Street. The fenced-in house set far back from the road, and the gate was locked. The house itself was big and grand, with a manicured lawn and well-trimmed bushes.

But the curtains were tightly closed, and Cornell saw no signs of life.

CHAPTER FIVE: BARELY A FIRE

On Monday, Cornell was walking to his classroom when he heard loud weeping from inside the teacher's lounge.

So he popped inside to take a look, just in case it was a wailing ghost.

It wasn't. Just some of the teachers.

"It's terrible," Mrs. English teacher cried.

"Madam, what's terrible?" Cornell asked.

Mrs. English teacher wiped her eyes with her handkerchief. "Bethany. They found her dead in her house."

"Dead? In her house?

"Yes!" Miss Librarian sobbed. "She died in a terrible house fire."

"When did this happen?"

"Last night!" Mrs. English teacher cried

just as Miss Librarian cried, "This morning!"

"That's very strange," Cornell said. "I didn't hear any fire trucks. I didn't hear an ambulance. Where does she live?"

"In a house," Mrs. English teacher said.

"In one of the neighborhoods," Miss Librarian said.

Both teachers hurried out of the lounge, whispering to each other.

Cornell walked away, hands in pockets, deep in thought. It had rained Saturday night, all day Sunday, and all last night and early this morning. How could Bethany's house burn down? Why didn't the rain put out the fire? Why hadn't he heard any emergency vehicles?

He had just reached his science classroom when Mr. Principal's voice boomed over the loudspeaker: "Professor Cornell Dyer, please come to the office right away."

So Cornell turned around, stopping first at the cafeteria vending machine to buy a can of orange drink and a bag of potato chips.

And then he noticed the school had quite a few changes since Friday night.

The leaky ceiling was fixed.

Paint was slapped here and there.

Missing tiles were replaced.

But the pool was closed.

"Professor, thank you for coming right away," Mr. Principal said when Cornell came into his office and sat down. "I have terrible news. Our science teacher has died. We'd like to hire you full-time right away."

"What happened?" Cornell said.

"I told you," Mr. Principal said. "She died."

"How did she die?"

"Why is that important?

"Because I heard she died in a house fire. But I didn't hear any emergency vehicles, just lots and lots of rain."

Mr. Principal bowed his head. Just outside his window, Cornell saw two garbagemen emptying the garbage.

Mr. Principal raised his head.

"So Bethany actually had a tiny fire in her stove while cooking," Mr. Principal said. "The fire caused her to have a heart attack. When she fell, she broke all her bones. So we need to replace her right away."

"When did she come home? I thought she was still missing."

"I finally talked to her on Friday night," Mr. Principal said. "She had broken her arm and couldn't answer the phone. Her old bones were very calcium-deficient. Last year, she tripped and broke her leg. She wouldn't even shake hands with people. Shaking hands might break her fingers."

"What is her address?" Cornell said.

"Why?" Mr. Principal asked.

"I'm a super supernatural super sleuth," Cornell said. "The stories are not lining up. I think something else happened to Bethany. I want to look for clues."

"No need, Professor," Mr. Principal said. "Bethany was very old. And the soup burned These things just happen. We want to hire you right away."

Mr. Principal slid a piece of paper to Cornell.

"Here is our offer," Mr. Principal said. "We spare no expense in educating our two hundred and thirty-two students. Oh, and there is a house for sale on Reed Street."

Cornell's eyes bulged. He could buy ten new motor homes every month on this salary.

"You will also receive a membership to our country club," Mr. Principal said. "We can introduce you to the right people. They will make your life better. We care about our teachers very much."

Except for Bethany, Cornell thought.

Aloud he said, "I will think about it."

"Please take you your time, Professor. We're not interviewing other teachers. We're only interested in you."

As Cornell rose to leave, he noticed a clean square on the floor with a dusty outline.

"Where's the filing cabinet?" Cornell asked.

"It's in the basement," Mr. Principal said. "We're remodeling, you know. Things are getting moved around."

Cornell slowly walked back to his classroom. As he walked, he peeked through the windows of the other classrooms. Some classrooms still had skeletons. And some only had empty poles.

Suddenly, Mr. Principal's voice boomed over the loudspeaker: "Attention, swim team. A crack was found over the weekend and the pool drained out. Practices are canceled until we fix the pool."

Cornell sped downstairs to the pool. In the hall, workmen were scraping tiles and painting the walls.

"I want to see the pool," Cornell said.

One workman shook his head. "You can't. It's cracked."

"It's dangerous," another workman echoed.

Just then, Mr. Principal appeared.

"Professor, you may not see the pool," Mr. Principal. "The pool has a crack."

.So Cornell went to his class and taught about skin and bone.

Amy raised her hand. "Will you teach us about animals, too?"

Jeff raised his hand. "Our old science teacher loved animals."

Diane raised her hand. "She loved elephants and zebras, and giraffes and tigers."

Mikey raised his hand. "She told us stories about the times she and her husband went to Africa."

The students all talked very loudly, over the roar of the motor from the garbage truck just outside the window.

Finally, it was time for lunch. Cornell helped himself to half a dozen corn dogs, a heaping pile of French fries, and three giant peanut butter cookies.

Cornell took his tray to the teacher's lounge. But the other teachers did not let him eat in peace.

"Will you take the teaching job?" Mr. Math Teacher asked. "It's a good opportunity."

"You know, there's a house for sale on Reed Street," Mrs. English teacher said.

"It's been empty for a long time," Miss Librarian said.

After the final bell rang, Cornell hurried downstairs to the pool. The door was locked, chained, and bolted.

One worker stood near a ladder polishing a light bulb on his shirt.

"Excuse me," Cornell said. "Do you have a key to the pool?"

"Sorry," the man said as he put his foot on the first step of the ladder. "I have to change this light bulb. I'm really, really busy."

Fuming, Cornell stomped out the front door and to his motor home just as a garbage truck pulled into the parking lot.

"Enough!" Cornell shouted.

Cornell waited with the motor running until the garbage truck emptied the dumpster and drove out of the parking lot. Then Cornell vroomed after it.

He passed the school grounds and the country club. The garbage truck picked up speed, with Cornell keeping pace. They drove over the hills. under the viaducts, and closer and closer to the Sunnystorm's downtown.

The garbage truck sped through a green light and then another green light and then another green light. Cornell and his motor home stayed right behind it.

Right turns, left turns, two more green lights, faster and faster and faster. The garbage truck did not stop to pick up garbage.

Cornell approached the center of town and the river. Tugboats glided across the water as if they hadn't any worries.

The garbage truck zoomed through a green light, which quickly turned yellow. Cornell floored the gas pedal, and three people stepped into the intersection.

Cornell slammed on the brakes and screeeeeeched to a stop.

The people smiled and waved as they kept strolling across the street.

"Sorry!" one called out.

"We didn't see you!" another shouted.

The light turned green. Cornell hit the gas.

The garbage truck bounced over the bridge.

Suddenly, the gates came down, and the bridge went up.

Cornell squealed to a stop.

Fuming, Cornell watched the bridge rise and the garbage truck drive away and out of sight.

CHAPTER SIX: 311 REED STREET

Fifty-six days later, on a Tuesday, Cornell stood in front of the chalkboard, drawing pictures of skeletons, and thinking about garbage trucks.

He still had not accepted the full-time teaching job.

The school was still being remodeled.

But each time Mr. Principal said, "That's OK, Professor. Just take your time. And don't forget, there's a really nice house on Reed Street. It's been empty a long time."

But then, two things happened that made this Tuesday different from the other Tuesdays.

One, Mr. Math teacher stopped Cornell in the hall during Cornell's break.

"May I buy you an orange drink and a bag of potato chips?" Mr. Math Teacher asked in his gravelly voice.

"Why?" Cornell asked.

Mr. Math Teacher blushed. He drew circles on the floor with his toe.

"Because I was rude," Mr. Math teacher finally said. "Because you've worked here five-six days, and we've never sat and talked.

But as soon as Cornell settled at a table with Mr. Math teacher, each with a can of orange drink and a big bag of potato chips, Mr. Math Teacher said, "Have you considered teaching full-time? You're really the best person for the job. Oh, and there's a house for sale on Reed Street. Been empty a long time."

Cornell snatched his bag and can and marched back to his classroom, just in time to see a garbage truck drive into the parking lot.

He made up his mind

At lunch time, Cornell headed straight for Mr. Principal's office. He almost bumped into the receptionist. She was carrying a new cactus plant for her shelf. The shelf was filled with lots of cacti plants – as well as orchids and ginseng.

"Sorry," Cornell said.

A few second later, Cornell was standing in front of Mr. Principal's desk and saying, "I'll take that full-time job."

"Fantastic!" Mr. Principal cried. "And

guess what? My realtor friend is visiting me today."

"Did someone call my name?" Mr. Realtor said as he walked into the office.

Mr. Principal smiled. "Professor Dyer has agreed to stay in Sunnystorm and teach all the sciences classes. But he needs a place to live."

"Would you like to see a really nice house on Reed Street?" Mr. Realtor said. "It's been empty a long time."

"Of course," Cornell said. "What's the address?"

"Three-eleven Reed Street." Mr. Realtor said with a big smile.

Cornell paid cash for the house because Sunnystorm School was paying him so much money.

In fact, the school board offered to pay for all the furnishings, too.

"We want to help," Mr. Principal said. "Because we care about education. And don't worry about the empty boxes. We have people who take out the garbage."

Cornell's new home had big rooms and high ceilings. It had an extra-long and extra-wide garage for his motor home.

The house was filled with maple wood blinds, maple wood furniture, maple wood bannisters and maple wood frames around the heavy oil landscapes hanging on the walls. Cornell also had ivory sculptures and ivory wall decorations.

He had a large grand piano made out of the finest maple wood.

He had a new pool table made out of maple wood.

He had shelves full of dominoes.

Cornell stayed up until past midnight that first night in his new home. He was thinking about the strange clues while listening to his favorite Wagnerian opera.

But as Cornell finally settled into bed, he heard a whisper.

Now this wasn't a person's whisper.

It was the whisper of a wind through a crack around an improperly sealed window.

The whisper was annoying. The whisper kept Cornell awake.

So Cornell grabbed his cashmere robe from one of his walk-in closets and a real flashlight out of one of his maple wood dressers.

Then he lumbered down the spiral staircase, with stairs and bannisters as ivory white as his piano keys.

Cornell looked all over that big house. But he could not find the whisper. He ran his hand around all the windows and along the doors.

Nothing.

He tapped on the walls and flattened his ear against the wall, listening for whispers.

Nothing.

Finally he pushed on all the walls.

Nothing.

Except for the wall behind the stairs. That wall opened up on hinges.

Cornell stepped behind the wall and felt the cool whisper.

He saw rows of shelves made from maple wood covering a hidden.

He saw a sliver of light from behind the top shelf.

So Cornell padded out to the motor home in his slippers and robe to find a screwdriver, and then he padded back inside. He unscrewed every screw that held every shelf in place. He stacked every shelf against a wall and then pocketed the screwdriver.

He pushed on the wall where the light seeped through it. That wall moved aside to reveal a circular opening, much like a small laundry chute.

Cornell snapped on his flashlight..

The passageway was filled with thick layers of gravel. Cornell heard, "drip, drip, drip" from far away.

So Cornell carefully squeezed into the chute, and he didn't lose a slipper. He crawled down the slope through pebbles and dust, never minding the cashmere robe because supernatural super sleuths on an important mission can't worry about those things.

Finally Cornell reached the bottom of the chute, where a little handcart was parked. And beyond the handcart was a long, dark passageway.

So Cornell climbed onto the cart and tried the handles, but nothing happened.

He shone his light all over the cart and found a green button with the words "ON."

Cornell pressed the button and chugged away.

CHAPTER SEVEN: MIDNIGHT ESCAPADE

The cart continued to pick up speed until Cornell reached the end of the line, which was a door.

Cornell heard people yelling, machines grinding, and boats tooting, all beyond the door.

Boats?

Cornell climbed out of the cart, carefully, so he wouldn't lose a slipper. Then he snapped off his flashlight and quietly opened the door.

The door led to a narrow walkway near the ceiling. Only a metal railing kept the walker safe from drowning in the water below.

Boats glided in one way and out the other.

Men loaded objects in and out of the boats and shouted to each other.

The man in the center of the commotion yelled the loudest and the most. He wore a slouched hat. He leaned on a maple wood cane. He smoked a cigar.

"Hurray up! Move faster!" the man barked. "Daylight's a 'comin'!"

Cornell put the flashlight in his mouth and gripped the handrail. Just beyond the mouth of the boathouse, garbage trucks pulled in and out of the parking lot.

"Yep, we're right on track," a familiar voice below Cornell and behind Cornell said.

So Cornell shimmied backwards – the walkway was too narrow for turning around – and glanced down..

"The timing is good," Mr. Principal said. "He finally took the job. And we finished the pool."

Out, Cornell thought. I need to get out.

Cornell inched backward some more. He reached for the door. And then…

The screwdriver slipped out of his pocket and hit the floor with a clinkety, clinkety, clinkety, clinkety-clinkety CLINK!

The people stopped moving.

The tugboat stopped tooting and tugging.

The garbage trucks stopped garbaging.

The old man screamed, "Get up there!"

Cornell softly closed the door behind him. He jumped onto the car.

He pressed and pressed and pressed the green button. The cart chugged faster and faster and faster.

Finally Cornell was at the end. He leapt out of the cart.

He quickly crawled up the gravely, dusty chute, scraping his bare knees raw.

He opened the door; he shut the door.

He hung the shelves as best he could without the screwdriver.

He flew out of the closet and tripped up the stairs two and three at a time, losing both slippers.

He threw on a shirt and a pair of shorts and splashed water on his face and hair just as he heard the DING-DONG of the doorbell.

Cornell jogged downstairs and opened the door, huffing and puffing.

Two garbagemen stood on his front porch.

"It's my workout time," Cornell gasped. "It's a scientific fact that the blood flows better after..."

Cornell noticed the large bare spot in the living room,. His piano was missing.

"We're so sorry to bother you," one garbageman said. "But do you have any garbage to throw away?"

"No garbage tonight," Cornell puffed.

"Are you OK?" the other garbage man said. "The house has been empty for a while."

"I'm fine," Cornell panted.

The garbage men looked at each other.

They smiled. They nodded.

"Well, then, good niiight," they said in a Peter Lorre voice.

Cornell shut the door and sank to the floor.

CHAPTER EIGHT: SECRET OF THE FRAME

The piano was back the next morning.

Well, not *the* piano.

But *a* piano.

This piano was a slightly smaller piano with slightly darker wood.

However, the ivory sculptures were gone.

The wall hangings were gone.

And one box of dominoes was gone, too.

The school had also changed.

The "new" floors looked like the old floors, just shinier.

The lockers were shiner, too, but they had the same old scratchers. The maple wood office door looked new, but it still creaked.

The scaffolding and ladders were gone.

The workmen were gone.

The pool was open.

Cornell examined the enormous pool on his lunch break. The water was shimmery clear. The blue and white tile shone with newness.

But something was missing.

That "something" small. But supernatural super sleuths notice even the smallest of the smallest of missing details.

Way in the corner in the shallow end…

Right above the water where the little heart that said J+A should be was…

Nothing.

The pool had no little heart.

Cornell took out is Tile-O-Magnify-Atic magnifying glass and peered closely at the tile.

Eureka!

The pattern was slightly different, too.

Cornell scratched his greasy uncombed curls, and the gears in his head cranked.

Sunnystorm School had not repaired the pool. It had replaced the pool.

Why would the school keep the old lockers but replace a perfectly good pool?

Cornell must find out.

So that night, Cornell switched on few lights in the house, to look like he was home. Then he tiptoed back to school through the woods with his supplies: brushing kit, microscope, and snacks.

Cornell was crossing he school parking lot when he heard a noise. He ducked behind a bush near front door. A garbage truck whizzed past.

But Cornell was not surprised.

"Ready, Skelly?" Cornell whispered.

"Yippers! Skelly whispered back.

Soon Cornell was roaming Sunnystorm School, inspecting every item in every classroom with his dusting kit and microscope. He wasn't just looking for fingerprints. He was looking for pieces of raw materials, too.

Cornell saved his classroom for last. He dusted and inspected everything, including the were the world map. He only had one item left to inspect: Bethany's desk.

Cornell carefully took apart the frame of young Bethany on the safari. He slid out the photo – and found a note taped to its back.

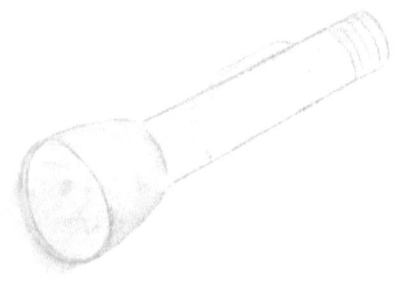

CHAPTER NINE: MEETING AT MIDNIGHT

Cornell unfolded the note and read: *It happens tomorrow at midnight.*

Tomorrow. At midnight.

Was this an old note? A new note? What was supposed to happen? And would it happen tomorrow at midnight?

Cornell dusted the note with his dusting kit. Then he reassembled the picture frame. And then he tiptoed home with his supplies and samples.

He stayed awake half the night studying his evidence. Finally he cried, "Eureka!"

As soon as school ended for the day, Cornell hurried to the principal's office.

"I've signed the paperwork," Cornell lied.

"But I forgot it at home. I'll bring it tonight at..."

Cornell blinked.

The chair in Mr. Principal's office still had the faded paisley cushions. But the wood on its arms, back, and legs wasn't nicked. Neither was the wood on Mr. Principal's desk. Or the wood on the picture frames.

"Tonight is not good for me," Mr. Principal said, "I have a very important meeting. Just bring the paperwork with you to school tomorrow." He picked up the phone. "Excuse me, Professor. I must make a phone call."

Well, Cornell had to make a phone call, too.

As Cornell left, he noticed the bare shelves in Miss Receptionist's office. Her plants were gone.

I knew it, Cornell thought.

That night, Cornell switched on few lights in the house, to look like he was home. Then he tiptoed back to school through the woods with his supplies and snacks.

The school was dark, except for the glint of a moving flashlight. Cornell was right on time.

He jimmied up a window with his jimmying tool. Then he climbed into the school.

Cornell switched on his ghost flashlight and ran up the stairs to his classroom, where Skelly let him in. Cornell crouched by the desk and waited.

Shortly after midnight, the door opened. Cornell leaped out and cried, "Gotcha!"

CHAPTER TEN: TALE OF TWINS

But Mr. Principal simply turned on the lights.

"But did you?" Mr. Principal said. "Or did I get you?"

Something jabbed Cornell in his back.

He whirled around.

There stood the old man from the boathouse with his cigar. The old man jabbed Cornell with his cane a second time.

But Cornell just laughed.

"I solved the mystery," Cornell bragged. "You got rid of Bethany. You stole her money. You use garbage trucks to move good material out of the school building and bring bad material into it."

The old man and Mr. Principal chuckled.

"You're somewhat right and mostly wrong, Professor," Mr. Principal said.

"You're a terrible sleuth, Professor!" the old man sneered.

Cornell crossed his arms. "So explain yourselves. Clearly, you've trapped me."

"Gladly," Mr. Principal said. "We're finishing up here tonight, anyway."

The old man snorted. "It's stupid to tell him."

"Why not?" Mr. Principal shrugged. "He can't spill our secrets."

"First question," Cornell said. "Why did you hurt a sweet old lady who loved teaching kids?"

The old man laughed and laughed. "She hated teaching!"

"Prove it," Cornell said.

The old man slid off his hat. His hair was white, curled, and topped with a bow. He, well, she, gave a little curtsy. "Meet the science teacher."

"Wow!" Cornell said. "You sure fooled me! No one ever fools me. May I shake your hand?"

"Certainly."

The science teacher held out her hand. Cornell gave it a firm shake.

"You fool!" Mr. Principal cried.

Mr. Principal lunged at the science teacher, but it was too late.

"Just as I thought," Cornell said. "You're not Bethany Ann Calloswick. Bethany could not shake hands. Her bones were calcium-deficient bones. Who are you?"

"I am Bethany's twin sister, Beverly Wonderbuilt," the old man who was not an old man or a science teacher said. "Mr. Principal is my son."

"We didn't hurt my Aunt Bethany at all," Mr. Principal said coolly. "She and her husband died in Africa many years ago."

"Then why impersonate her?" Cornell asked.

"Two reasons," Mr. Principal said. "One, she was a very good teacher, and the students loved her. Aunt Bethany was happiest in this classroom. She never wanted to leave."

"A likely story!"

Mr. Principal shrugged. "As I told you, we support education here at Sunnystorm. We could not break the students' hearts."

"Fine. What was the other reason?"

"Poaching," Beverly said.

"Poaching?" Cornell asked.

Beverly lit a cigar and tapped the ashes on the floor. "Yes, poaching. Bethany's husband was very rich. He was also a photographer. They both loved animals and the environment. They took many trips around the world, especially to Africa, to take pictures. After Bethany and her husband died, we saw our chance."

"Your chance?" Cornell asked.

Mr. Principal nodded. "The people of Sunnystorm have always worked very hard. But they never made much money. The town struggled to survive. Our industry wasn't good. We could not educate our children well."

"So we invented an industry," Beverly said.

"A poaching industry," Cornell accused.

"Yes," Mr. Principal said. "As material comes into our town, we move it around town and then move it out of town for resale."

"We started with ivory from elephant tusks," Beverly bragged. "When we saw how easy it was, we branched out into…"

"Furs, cacti, ginseng, orchids, diamonds, leather, and rare maple wood," Cornell said.

Beverly scowled. "Well, aren't you the smarty pants."

"He certainly is!" a familiar voice from the doorway said.

Cornell turned to look. There stood Mr. History Teacher and the two garbage truck drivers who came to Cornell's house that one night.

"Meet Special Agent A, Special Agent B, and Special Agent C," Cornell said, pointing to each agent as he named them.

"Nice work, Professor," Mr. History

Teacher (Special Agent A) said as he snapped handcuffs onto Mr. Principal's wrists.

Special Agent B nodded. "Well done, indeed." And then he snapped a pair of handcuffs on Beverly's strong wrists.

"You tricked me!" Mr. Principal finally cried. "You told me to hire the Professor!"

Cornell turned to Mr. Principal and Beverly. "Actually, the agents called me first and told me to expect your call. But I didn't know them until they taught me the secret sign. Agents, take them away!"

"The secret sign?" Mr. Principal looked perplexed. "What secret sign."

Cornell grinned and said in a Peter Lorre voice, "Goood niiiiight."

EPILOGUE

The final bell for the final class of Cornell's final day of teaching finally rang.

The students dashed out the door. Cornell packed his briefcase, ready to get on the road.

Mr. Janitor walked through the door. "Guess what I found!"

And then Mr. Janitor brought in something that belonged in the science classroom. It was the skeleton that had disappeared on Cornell's first day of teaching.

"I was cleaning out Mr. Principal's office and found it in his closet," Mr. Janitor said. "I wonder how it got in there."

"Very strange," Cornell agreed.

"Can you give me a hand?" Mr. Janitor asked. "I don't want to break it. The bones are very calcium deficient."

That's when Cornell noticed the skeleton's commanding eye sockets and steady gaze.

Now most skeletons look as if they're grinning. But this skeleton seemed to smile right at Cornell.

Cornell carefully helped Mr. Janitor rehang the skeleton on the pole.

"She sure looks happy," Mr. Janitor said. "Almost as if she's glad to be back. Maybe she missed her classroom."

Mr. Janitor winked.

"Maybe," Cornell said.

A student rushed up. "Mr. Janitor, have you seen the world famous supernatural super sleuth Cornell Dyer?"

"I'm right here," Cornell said. "I am he who specializes in Amulets, Fortune-Telling (with and without cards), Ghost-Hunting, Horoscopes, Numerology, Palm-Reading, Potions, Séances, Spells, Vampire-Slaying, controlling zambicallo populations, and deactivating Moravian pink goblins, cold whispers, and classroom skeletons with..."

"You have a letter!"

Cornell snatched the envelope, ripped it open, and read:

My dearest Professor,

I have been looking for you for a long time.

I had to use the last of my magic in a bottle to find you.

Please come with haste for I am running out of time. An old haunt has returned.

I have not seen it, but I can feel it. I feel it lurking in the dark shadows around unsuspecting corners.

A coldness comes at night that leaves the grass frosted and dead.

I hear it. The faint howls grow stronger in the night.

I have stayed where I've been all these years protecting the thing that needs protecting but now, more than ever, I need an extra pair of hands.

There is a door, and behind the door is a hallway. It's windowless and dark and all manner of wicked creatures move about stopping me from advancing. This hallway has never know light.

We must join together again. One must survive if the others fail.

My dear man Wipston is with me. We are preparing for our last mystery.

Please join us my friend.

"For by the moonlight we dance,
"And from fingertips flow romance,
"Like a river springing to life,
"The dogs snarl and bite,
        "To keep her safe at night,
      "But even still there is no chance,
      "For the darkness buries the day,
       "The priests forget how to pray,
  "And the ground shakes with the souls of
                the dead,
          "The schoolteacher weeps,
          "For the husband she seeks,
         "That man who went off to war,
             "He left with a grin,
              "Spread over his chin,
            "To be seen nevermore."

He is coming.
Sherman A. Holmes

THE FACTS IN THE FICTION

Poaching is when people kill animals, fish, or plants without permission and then sell them to make money.

Items people poach include ivory from elephant tusks, maple leaf wood, green cacti, purple orchids, white ginseng, tortoise, diamonds, and abalone, a type of sea creature.

Money laundering is when people take the money they made illegally and make it look as if they made it legally.

In Sunnystorm, people poached the above items, turned them into real objects, and then sold them to people who bought them for the raw materials.

Calcium is a mineral that's needed for strong bones. The scientific term for bones that are calcium deficient is osteoporosis.

Having a skeleton hanging in a classroom is a trope that's often used in stories.

A trope is word, phrase, or picture that's used in storytelling.

The names "Milton Motel" and the "Wonderbuilt" family are parodies of a family hotel (Hilton Hotel) and a famous family (Vanderbuilt).

A parody is an imitation of the real thing that's sometimes used in art.

For more information about the Hilton Hotel, visit hilton.com.

For more information about the Vanderbuilts, visit biltmore.com.

About the Author

Denise M. Baran-Unland is the author of the BryonySeries supernatural/literary trilogy for young and new adults, the Adventures of Cornell Dyer chapter book series for grade school children and the Bertrand the Mouse series for young children.

She has six adult children, three adult stepchildren, fourteen total grandchildren, six godchildren, and four cats.

She is the co-founder of WriteOn Joliet and previously taught features writing for a homeschool coop, with the students' work published in the co-op magazine and The Herald-News in Joliet.

Denise blogs daily and is currently the features editor at The Herald-News. To read her feature stories, visit theherald-news.com. For more information about Denise's fiction and to follow her on social media, visit bryonyseries.com.

Sue Midlock lives in Illinois with her husband and has been writing for 10 years. She started writing when the book "Twilight" first came out and fell in love with the paranormal genre.

Since then, she has written and finished her Rosewood Trilogy and just recently her anniversary edition, "Forever," which is the first book re-written for adults.

Her most recent releases are "Southern Shorts," which is an anthology of short stories about Dry Prong, Louisana and "Night Games

Timothy Baran enjoys cooking on professional and home levels. He also likes writing dark poetry and stories whose style mimics C. S. Lewis, his favorite author.

He is currently working on his first novel and a book of poetry.

But he especially loves his cat Midnight, whom he raised from a kitten.